The Blizzard Wizard

Story by
Lynn Plourde

Illustrated by
John Aardema

Down East

"No snow?" sighed the kids one early winter day.

"No snow," said the Blizzard Wizard. "I can't find my snow spell. It must be here somewhere."

"But how can we make snowmen without big round balls of snow?"

"So sorry," apologized the Blizzard Wizard. He knew a winter without snow was like a birthday cake without candles.

"Let me try to make some snow. I'm sure I can remember a few words from the spell."

The Blizzard Wizard raced outside and wildly waved his wand:

"White and fluffy.

"Fluffy and white.

"Rah-rah-rah—sis-boom-BAAAAAAA!"

It worked! White and fluffy things began falling from the sky!

"Hooray!" shouted the kids as they made BAAAAAA-eautiful snowmen.

"Still no snow?" sighed the kids one mid-winter day.

"Still no snow," said the Blizzard Wizard. "I hope to find my snow spell any second now. I've even had my owls searching, but they don't give a hoot."

"But how can we go sledding without slippery snow?"

"So sorry," apologized the Blizzard Wizard. He knew a winter without snow was like riding a bike without wheels.

He frantically turned the pages of one of his books, checking every single "S" spell. "Here's a *slippery* spell!" he announced.

The Blizzard Wizard climbed atop the kids' favorite sledding hill and chanted:

"Slippery, slippery.
"Bunches and bunches.
"Make this place aPEELing!"

It worked! Slippery things suddenly covered the hill.

"Hooray!" shouted the kids, who didn't need their sleds to go sliding on the slippery, sloppy, floppy peels.

"Still, still no snow?" sighed the kids one late winter day.

"Still, still no snow," said the Blizzard Wizard. "I've even looked behind all the invisible things in my supply closet."

"But how can we build snow forts without sticky snow?"

"So sorry," apologized the Blizzard Wizard. He knew a winter without snow was like eating macaroni without cheese.

He checked his supply closet for some sticky ingredients, shoving aside his invisible potions, flying lotions, and gizzard notions.

"Aha! These should work!" shouted the Blizzard Wizard.

He stirred sticky ingredients into his cauldron.

"Sticky, wicky.
"Stucky, wucky.
"Syrupy, wyrupy—WHAM!"

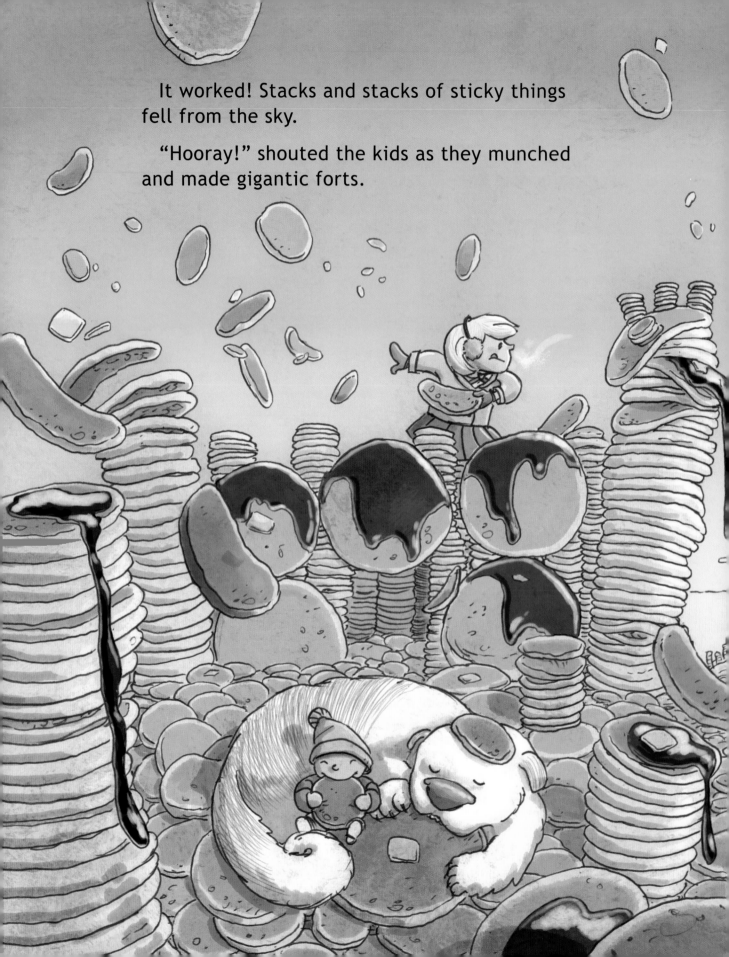

It worked! Stacks and stacks of sticky things fell from the sky.

"Hooray!" shouted the kids as they munched and made gigantic forts.

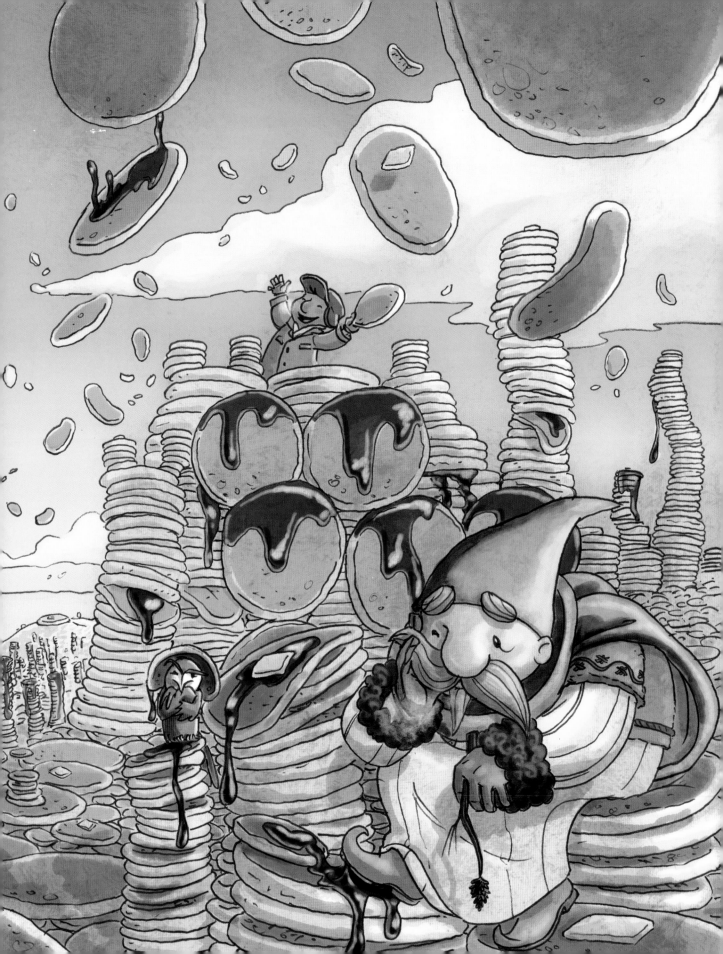

Still, still, still no snow . . .

But it didn't matter. It was spring.

"Thanks for the fun winter, Blizzard Wizard." said the kids. "But we hope that next year you'll find your spell and make some *real* snow."

"Thanks for being understanding," said the Blizzard Wizard. "I promise I'll look for my snow spell every single second." After all, he knew a winter without snow was like a rainbow without colors.

One mid-summer day, the kids invited the Blizzard Wizard to join them at the beach.

"But I haven't found my snow spell."

"Come on. You deserve *one* day off," said the kids. "And you still have the rest of the summer and all of fall to search."

When they set foot on the beach, the kids shouted, "Last one in is a rotten wizard!"

They grabbed the Blizzard Wizard by his robe and tugged him toward the water's edge.

R-i-i-i-i-i-i-i-i-p!

"Oh no! We tore your robe," said the kids.

"Don't worry. I'm wearing a bathing suit underneath. I'll fix my robe later with a breathtaking thread-making spell."

The Blizzard Wizard wiggled out of his robe and slung it aside. As it landed on the sand, one of the kids saw something white inside.

"Is that a tag?" she asked. "What size do wizard robes come in?"

"No, it's not a tag," said the Blizzard Wizard. "Wizard robes are one size magically fits all." He glanced down and shouted, "My snow spell! That's where I pinned it—safe inside my robe, so I wouldn't lose it."

"Hooray!" shouted the kids.

"SHOWTIME! SNOWTIME!" announced the Blizzard Wizard, as he checked his snow spell and began chanting magical words. After all, he knew it was never too late to make up for lost time, and the winter without snow had been like dancing without music.

A Blizzard

In this story the Blizzard Wizard was trying to make snow, but a blizzard is more than just snow. It also has winds higher than 35 miles per hour, which blow the snow around and make it hard to see (less than one-quarter mile visibility). For example, the Northeast Blizzard of 1978 on February 5 through 8 dumped up to 55 inches of snow and had winds of 65 miles per hour. It took six days for people to dig out from that blizzard!

If there *really* were a Blizzard Wizard, he would work year-round. When it's summer in the northern hemisphere (top half of the earth), it's winter in the southern hemisphere (bottom half of the earth), and vice versa. People in Australia celebrate Christmas during their summer.

Sometimes blizzards happen only in small areas. The moist air coming off one of the Great Lakes can cause a localized blizzard, also known as a snowburst, dumping as much as 11 inches of snow per hour. Cities such as Buffalo, Syracuse, and Rochester, New York, experience these lake-effect storms while places a few miles away escape the snow.

One of the BIGGEST blizzards, called the Great White Hurricane, was in March of 1888. It paralyzed the northeastern United States from March 11 through 14 and left snowdrifts 40 to 50 feet high! As a result of that storm, New York City started to build a subway system so everyone could get around even when it snowed.

# of Facts

The kids in this story wanted different kinds of snow—slippery for sledding and sticky for building snow forts. If snow falls when the temperature is near freezing (0 degrees Celsius, or 32 degrees Fahrenheit), it will be wet, heavy, and sticky. Sometimes sleet or freezing rain mixes with snow to make it icy and slippery. If snow falls when the temperature is well below freezing, it will be dry and powdery and blow around easily in the wind. It's a common myth that Eskimos have different names for different kinds of snow. They don't, but maybe we can invent our own names—how about *sneet* for snow and sleet mixed together, and *snuffy* for very fluffy snow?

Many people complain about the bad parts of a blizzard—the heavy snow, howling winds, dangerous driving—but a blizzard can be good. For example, in 2003, part of Colorado was experiencing an extreme drought. Then, in mid-March, a storm called the Drought-Busting Blizzard dumped three to seven feet of snow over a two-day period in the mountains. All that snow later melted and replenished the water supplies for nearby towns.

During the winter of 1963-64, the Blizzard Wizard worked overtime in author Lynn Plourde's home state of Maine. The first snowfall was on September 13, 1963, and the last occurred on June 17, 1964. So that winter lasted nine months!

If there really were a Blizzard Wizard, you might expect him to be especially busy in the Arctic (around the North Pole) and Antarctica (around the South Pole). Both poles are actually deserts, receiving only one to fifteen inches of snow a year. It's so cold at the poles that the snow and ice never completely melt, and the winds, which can blow as hard as 198 miles per hour, create blinding snowstorms with just a tiny bit of snow.

With love and thanks to Paul
for 25 magical years —LP

Story Copyright © 2010 by Lynn Plourde,
Illustrations © 2010 by John Aardema.
All rights reserved.
ISBN: 978-0-89272-789-6
Design by Rich Eastman
Printed in China

5 4 3 2 1

Library of Congress Cataloging-in-Publication Data

Plourde, Lynn.
    The Blizzard Wizard / story by Lynn Plourde ; illustrations by John Aardema.
        p. cm.
    Summary: The Blizzard Wizard has lost his snow spell, but he still attempts to provide
wintry fun for the boys and girls. Includes facts about winter, snow, and blizzards.
    ISBN 978-0-89272-789-6 (hardcover : alk. paper)
    [1. Wizards--Fiction. 2. Snow--Fiction. 3. Magic--Fiction.] I. Aardema, John, ill. II. Title.
PZ7.P724Bl 2010
[E]--dc22

                                                            2008051827

BOOKS·MAGAZINE·ONLINE
www.downeast.com

Distributed to the trade by National Book Network